Alexa Downs

an addyson investigations novel

by

Marie Garcia

Dedication

To my husband for letting me
complain about how things
were going.

Addyson Private Investigations

Kaula Dawkins

Adam Corning

Pami Simpson

Tabitha Johnson

Chapter 1

July 15, 2010

Shasta Mountains, Califoria

I was so glad that I'd taken a good, stiff shot of Jameson before I'd taken that test. I would have to try really hard to stop drinking.

I'd taken a good snort of cocaine two days ago. I liked heroin, too. I shot that stuff between my toes. No needle marks that way. Well, no visible needle marks.

"What are we going to do?" I asked.

Last month myself and two co-workers, Hope and Teri, had all hooked up with a hotel guest named Haden that was passing through the area. He had paid cash, up front. Then he left after a couple of days.

"I can't believe it," Hope said. "How could this have happened?"

"We all fucked that dick," Teri said, bluntly. "He knocked us all up. Apparently, my mother wasn't lying. One good fuck really *is* all it takes."

Hope Alvarez was one of the best housekeepers here at the Shasta Mountain Lodge. Teri Wilkinson was one of the best front desk clerks here. We'd all three made the mistake of fucking Haden. Though, he was really good.

"There was something off about it. I knew it the second he'd paid in cash."

Teri sighed. "It's not my fault that the two of you fucked him."

"Of course not. That's on us. You never should have taken the cash."

"It was for three weeks, paid in full! Plus a deposit. You gave me a bonus!"

I shook my head. "I'm sorry. What are we going to do? The lodge can't afford for us all to take maternity leave at the same the time!"

"Alexa, do you know anything about Haden? Did you say you spent more time with him?"

"Well, I admit, I did snoop while he was in the shower. He his name is Haden Delta and he lives in Vancouver, Washington. I found a business card. He's an elementary school principal. I called the school. Get this, they think he's dead!"

My two friends looked at me in disbelief. "What?"

"Apparently he was shot outside the home he and his girlfriend share."

"Girlfriend?"

"He never said he had a girlfriend!"

I looked at them. "Did you ask? Either of you? I know I didn't. I just wanted to fuck him after Teri described him."

"Well, no," Hope said. "I just started cleaning his room. He came up behind me. I felt his dick against my ass and when he asked me to say yes, I did."

Teri shook her head. "Honestly, it didn't even cross my mind. I kissed him and things just happened."

"Then we really can't blame him, can we?"

"No."

"I guess not."

"Seriously though, what are we going to do?"

"We'll start by saving money. We'll move in together. Share expenses."

"That's ridiculous."

"Why, do you plan on not keeping the baby? My parents left me a large house. There's more than enough room. I'm always lonely there anyway. Move in with me. We'll split utilities, groceries. Child care costs."

Hope and Teri looked at me.

"What?"

Chapter 2

"Do you need to work?" Hope asked.

"Are you rich?" Teri wondered.

I shook my head. "My parents left me a house," I replied. "That's all."

"You said it was a 'large' house. How large?"

I shrugged. "Six bedrooms, six bathrooms. Gourmet kitchen. Walk-in pantry. Three car garage."

"You *are* rich!"

"No. My parents were. They didn't leave me any money. The money that there is is in a trust that keeps the house running. They made sure that there was money to pay all the bills and upkeep. It's run by an executor to keep the house maintained. I do *have* to work."

"I'll move in with you," Hope said. "I hate living by myself anyway."

Teri shrugged. "Why not?"

"Great. I'll give you my address and you can start moving right away. You're going to love the house. It's a split-level. There are two bedrooms and two bathrooms per level. It's almost like separate apartments anyway."

They nodded and I wrote down the address.

Chapter 3

August 1, 2014

Hope, Teri, and I had been living together for a few weeks now. Maybe less. We all decided to go to the same OB/GYN and keep our appointments together whenever possible.

So, far I'd been able to hide my drug and alcohol addictions. It was very difficult to do. I really didn't want to be pregnant. I was selfish. I didn't even want my job. My parents had told me before they died that they didn't care how I lived my life, but if I was going to do drugs they wouldn't support the habit.

They also pointed out that I would never have the life that I wanted if I continued my drug and alcohol use. More on that later. It will make sense soon enough. Hopefully. I mean nothing made sense to me right now.

Our babies would be raised together. I had told my grandparents about the baby and they weren't happy. They said that my parents wouldn't be happy with me. That they'd be very disappointed in me.

I disagreed.

I spoke with my parents often, prior to their deaths. I'd spoken to my parents about how I had decided to live my life. They told me that as long as I was happy that was all they had cared about. I told them that I wanted kids and planned on adopting all the kids that I wanted. That I'd be a single mother. That was why they'd left me the house. So, I could work or not.

"Are you okay?" Teri asked.

Hope had left for the weekend to spend time with her family in Oregon. Klamath Falls, I believe it was. She'd wanted to see them before the weather turned bad. Living in the mountains the weather was unpredictable. I think she wasn't ready to tell them that she was pregnant and going to be a single, unwed mother. I think she wanted to see them before she started to show.

I was sitting at the foot of my bed. I'd been crying. I though that'd been quiet.

"No," I replied.

"Can I come in?"

"Sure."

Teri took a seat next to me. "What's wrong?"

"I don't know. Stupid hormones."

"Alexa, you don't always have to be so strong."

"Yes, I do."

She looked at me. "Why?"

"I'm the boss."

"Yes and you're a very good boss. Great, in fact, but we're not at work. We're at home and the three of us are in the same boat. We're going to be there for each other. Raise our kids together."

My phone rang, interrupting what I was going to say. "Hello?" I said, picking up my cell phone.

"Ms. Downs?" the voice asked.

"Yes?"

"I'm the nurse from your doctor's office. There was something off with your tests. Nothing bad. The doctor would like you to come back in."

"Of course. When?"

"Now, if you can."

"Sure. I can be there in about half an hour."

"Sure. That's fine."

I hung up and looked at Teri.

Great, I thought. *There is already something wrong with my baby.*

I needed to stop drinking and doing drugs right away.

"Wha..." Teri started, but her phone rang. It was the doctor.

Wait, if there was something medically wrong due to my drug use, then why did they call Teri in, too. That didn't make sense. Teri was a model employee. Never late. Always ready to help out wherever it was needed.

Maybe there was something genetically wrong with her baby. Teri and her family weren't close. She didn't even know a lot of her family. I think she was adopted.

Crap. Could Haden and Teri have been related? Could they be brother and sister and not even know it?

Chapter 4

Teri and I arrived at the doctor's office about half an hour later. We had asked the nurse to be seen together, which they accommodated.

"Oh!" the doctor said. "I didn't think that I'd be seeing the two of you at the same time."

"Our pregnancies are the result of a one night stand with the same man," Teri said.

"At separate times," I added. "We're in these pregnancies together."

"That's good."

"Why?"

"It's always good to have a support system."

I looked at the doctor. It had sounded like she was relieved. That didn't sound good. "Nancy, what is up with our tests?"

"It looks like you're both carrying twins. I want to run the tests again and do an ultrasound for the both of you."

"Twins?"

"How is that possible? There are no twins in my family."

"Does his?"

I shrugged. "There wasn't a lot of talking done."

"I see."

God, twins?

I really needed a shot of Jack or Jameson. Rum would work right now, too. What the fuck was I going to do with *two* babies? I might have been able to pawn one off on either Teri or Hope, but not *two*. Especially, since Teri was going to have two of her own.

I needed some cocaine or heroin. Maybe both. Anything to not feel like this right now. Anything to forget that I was pregnant. Anything to forget that I was pregnant with *twins*!

Maybe I could find Haden? He could take them, right?

* * *

Teri and I sat at the dining room table and stared at our uneaten food.

After the blood tests and the ultrasounds, the doctor had confirmed that we were both pregnant with twins. Their due dates were March of next year.

"What are the odds?" Teri asked, breaking the silence. "Seriously?"

"I don't know, but we need to get a hold of Hope," I said.

My phone rang and I picked it up from the table where it was sitting. I looked at the caller ID. "Hope."

"Put it on speaker."

"Hello?" Hope asked.

"Hi. We're both here. What's up?"

"The doctor just called me."

"I put you on speaker, if you couldn't tell. What did she say?"

"She mentioned redoing some of my tests." Hope was whispering. I knew I was right then. She didn't want her family to know. "I told her that I was out of town."

"We had to have tests, too."

"What? Why?"

"We're both pregnant with twins. You may want to get back sooner rather than later. Get in to see her as quick as possible."

"Got it. There is a bus tomorrow at noon. I'll be on it."

"See you tomorrow."

"Bye."

"Bye."

I looked at Teri and wondered if it were possible that all three of us would be pregnant with twins.

Chapter 5

March 6, 2011

"Push, Alexa, push," the doctor said. "The first baby is crowning!"

"It's too hard!" I exclaimed. "I can't."

"It's too late to do a C-section for the first baby. You have to push. You got this!"

I took a deep breath and pushed as hard as I could.

"It's a girl!"

She wasn't crying.

"Why isn't she crying? Is she okay?"

I killed her! I thought. *I killed her!*

The doctor handed her to the nurse. "She's okay. Mucus in the lungs. That's normal. The nurse can clear it."

"Are you sure?"

"Yes." The doctor returned to check me out, to see how much longer it would be until the second baby arrived. I still felt like I needed to push.

"Crap. No time to relax."

"What?"

"The second baby is already crowning. Push!"

I cried out as the contraction rushed through my body.

"Good." My baby girl cried finally. "It's a boy!"

My water broke at four o'clock in the morning and my twins, Bayley and Roman, were born between six o'clock and six thirty in the morning. They weighed six pounds and seven ounces each. Nineteen inches long.

Teri's water broke while she was driving me to the hospital with Hope in tow. Her twins, Aurora and Victoria, were born next. Between six forty-five and six fifty in the morning. They were five pounds and eight ounces. Twenty inches long.

Hope had the longest labor. As we waited for a room for me and for Teri, her water had broken. When she'd returned from Oregon, we found out that she was pregnant with triplets. Her active labor started at five o'clock in the morning and the last baby was delivered at ten o'clock in the morning. She refused to have them go in and do a C-section. Emilia Rose was born first and weighed five pounds two ounces. Nineteen inches long. Sadie Mallory was born second. She weighed five pounds eight ounces. Also, nineteen inches long. Donovan Haden was born last and thankfully, he wasn't the only boy in the group. He was six pounds and nineteen inches long.

The boys strongly resembled each other. So did the girls.

Teri's girls were darker, but then so was she. They were all beautiful and happy and healthy.

The three of us were tired. Exhausted. In pain. Full of happiness and bliss and worry.

Chapter 6

February 2, 2019

I couldn't take it anymore. These kids were whiny and needy. I felt like I was failing them daily. There had been at least two dozen times, if not more, that I couldn't feed them or get them new clothes for school. Since I was free of them sharing my body, not that it stopped me, but I deserved and had earned a decent fix.

I looked up a private investigator. Her name was Addyson Delta and she operated out of Vancouver. I had rented a small one bedroom hotel room in a town called Hazel Dell that had monthly, weekly, and nightly rates. I believe they even had hourly rates.

I tried to remember the address I'd seen on Haden's license, but couldn't. Hopefully, he was still in that area.

* * *

"You're doing what?" Teri demanded.

"I'm going to find their father," I replied. "Bayley, Roman, and I are going to Vancouver. I checked out a good private investigator."

"What about us?" Hope said.

"You're more than welcome to come with us; otherwise, I'll call as soon as I find out about him."

"When you find him, what are you going to say?"

I shrugged. "I don't know, but eight years is too long for these kids to not know their father. Keep the house, if you decide to stay. Don't worry about being kicked out. Okay? I'll check in."

"We can't stop you?"

"No. I already have a meeting set up in a couple of days. Her name is Addyson and she's got a top rating."

"Please, be safe."

"You, too."

I hugged them and went to grab the kids. There was no time like the present. We weren't far away and the kids could color to stay occupied for the six hours it would take to drive there.

Chapter 7

February 3, 2019
Portland, Oregon

During a brief conversation, Haden, had mentioned a hotel that he would frequent as a kid. Even though his family was close to home, they would always stop for an extra night away. I looked it up, but the name wasn't the same.

Bayley, Roman, and I stopped at the hotel in Delta Park. It was about ten minutes from Addyson's office. I didn't tell Teri or Hope that her last name was also Delta and that I didn't think the name was very common. Not in Vancouver. Not anywhere.

I had a feeling that Addyson Delta was Haden's wife.

I just hoped that she would help me. I also hoped that she wouldn't put off telling me where Haden was. I hoped that she would be honest enough to tell me who she was and that she wouldn't take my money for work that she didn't need to do.

I looked over and the twins were asleep. I crept into the bathroom and gathered my bathroom kit on the way. I had some cocaine and heroin in the bag.

I quietly closed the door and cut a line of cocaine. It felt good.

Then I took a shot of the Jameson that I had in my bad.

That was so good, too.

I was going to need all the courage that I could get. Especially with the feeling I had that Addyson was Haden's wife.

Chapter 8

The next day, I had found a day care that would let me drop off the kids even though I wasn't a resident and then I headed to see Addyson Delta.

"Welcome to *Addyson Investigations*," the male receptionist said. "How can I help you? Do you have an appointment?"

"Yes," I replied, suddenly nervous. "With Addyson. At ten."

"All right." He looked at his computer screen. "Ms. Downs?"

"Yes."

"Her previous meeting is running a little late. Could you please have a seat? I'll call you when she's ready."

"Sure."

I took a seat and mentally prepared myself to meet Haden's wife.

* * *

"Ms. Downs?" the receptionist called.

I looked up from my phone and answered, "Yes?"

"Addyson will see you now. Go down the hall. Two doors down on the left."

"Thank you." I followed his instructions and knocked on the closed door that I came to.

"Come in," a feminine voice called. "Ms. Downs?"

"Please, call me Alexa," I said, opening the door.

"Alexa." She smiled warmly. "Please come in and have a seat. Do you need a drink? Coffee? Tea? Soda?"

"No, thank you."

"How can I help?"

I took a deep breath. "Eight years ago, I had a one-night stand and I got pregnant. I worked at a hotel as a manager and when I found out that one of my clerks had taken a full cash payment, I went to speak to him about it. We hooked up."

God, I needed a snort of whiskey. Badly.

She was his wife. She had to be.

"Was he cute?"

"Very."

"Was he good? Big?"

I reddened. "Yes."

"Did you keep the baby?"

"Babies. It was twins, yes, I kept them."

"Boys? Girls?"

"One boy, Roman. One girl, Bayley."

"You weren't able to track him down until now?"

"I have an address, but it may be old. I snooped in his things while he was in the shower. He thought I was asleep. I know he's from Vancouver."

"Then why do you need me?"

"I want to make sure that he's still here before I go and ruin his life. He could be married and have other kids. He could not even like kids."

Addyson cocked her head. It looked like she was contemplating her next question, carefully. "Would it stop you from looking for him, if he was married? Had kids?"

I thought about it. I was pretty sure that I was talking to his wife. "No. My kids deserve there father, too."

"Of course. I'll do what I can to help you find him. What can you tell me about him? Description? Job?"

"He was about forty years old when we hooked up. So, I'd say he's close to fifty now. Weighs maybe 230 pounds. It's all muscle, at least, then from what I could tell there was no extra fat on him at all. Short brown hair, but not a buzz cut. About six feet two inches tall."

"Good. Good. Name?"

I took a deep, steadying breath again. My heart was in my throat. I'd been dreading this question. "Haden Delta."

I was looking at her when I said it and I saw her head jerk up. "What? Who?"

"Haden Delta. While was with me for one night at the hotel I'd worked at, he also had a night with two of my co-workers. Teri had twin girls named Aurora and Victoria. Hope had triplets. Two girls named Emilia Rose and Sadie Mallory. A little boy name Donovan Haden."

"What?"

I looked her. She wasn't going to say it. I could understand why. I'd just told her that her husband had slept with three different women eight years ago and that he had seven kids that neither of them had known about.

"Haden is your husband, isn't he?"

Addyson just looked at me like she hadn't heard me.

Chapter 9

Fuck! Fuck! I thought. *I knew it! This is why I didn't say anything to Hope and Teri.*

I needed a drink badly.

"Yes," Addyson said, finally. She had to visibly shake herself.

"I'm sorry," I replied. I meant it. "I don't want anything from him, financially. Neither do my friends. We just want our kids to know their father. Well, I do. I can't speak for them. They really didn't want me to come. I don't know why."

"Of course. Can you please take a seat in the lobby? I just need a minute. He didn't know?"

"I don't see how. I never told him."

She nodded.

I got up and left. I was actually afraid that she was going to call the cops on me, but I did as she asked and took a seat in the lobby.

* * *

Twenty minutes later, Haden walked into the lobby.

He looked over at me and then his eyes went wide. Then he ran down the hall. "Oh, God," he muttered. "Why did he have to be right?"

I didn't know what that last part was about, but the receptionists were looking at me.

Everyone was looking at me.

The phone rang at the desk and the female receptionist answered the phone. She glanced in my direction and said, "Yes, she is. Okay. Ms. Downs, Addyson will see you now."

I stood. "Thank you," I said.

I kept my head held high and my eyes forward. I couldn't take the stares.

Chapter 10

"I'm sorry," Addyson said, as I entered the office. "It caught me off guard."

"No, I'm sorry," I replied. "I never should have come. Hope and Teri were right."

"Please call them have them bring the kids up," Haden said.

"What?"

"Addyson and I would like you to bring your twins to the house today. They have a few siblings to meet. I'd also like to meet the other kids."

"Your friends' children do as well. Please call them. Then you and the kids can come over any time today."

I looked at Addyson. How could he have cheated on her? She's amazing.

Haden was nodding and Addyson was shaking her head.

"Sure. We can come by in about an hour, if that's okay?"

"That's fine."

I thanked them and left. I didn't want to press my luck

* * *

Haden and Addyson introduced me, Bayley, and Roman to their kids: Austin and Jackson and Melody. To Addyson's kids: Aria and Abby. Angela and Emerald. They had two other kids: Tessa and Sage, but they were in California.

Not long after that, Haden and Addyson left the living room for about twenty minutes only for her to leave the house completely.

Haden waited around and talked to the kids, but he was clearly distracted by her absence. He asked me to if I'd stay with the little ones and left. He returned and told me that he'd found her at her office. Then I asked him to watch Roman and Bayley.

I needed to talk to Addyson. I didn't want her to hate the kids.

Chapter 11

I knocked on Addyson's door. I needed to tell her why I was really here. That I was leaving the kids here. That I was a horrible mother.

"Come in," Addyson called, looking up. "Oh. Hello."

"I wanted to apologize," I said. That's not what I wanted to say. I'm such a fucking chicken.

"Apologize? For what, Alexa? Destroying my life? My faith in Haden?"

"Yes. I didn't know he was married."

She looked at her. "We weren't married at the time. It doesn't matter."

"Yes, it does."

"We had an open relationship and we have an open marriage."

"Oh, May I sit?"

Addyson nodded. "Sure."

I took a seat and tried to get comfortable.

"Look, I don't hate you. I don't hate your daughter or your son. I don't think they shouldn't see their father. I wish you had looked sooner."

"Then what?"

"I don't know. I think you and the kids should stay in town. I know a nice house for rent. If you need work, I can help with that, too."

"I don't know if that's a good idea."

"Listen, Haden missed eight years with Bayley and Roman. Don't let them miss another day. Not because of me. We can go to the house. At least take a look."

I was sure that looked even more uncomfortable than I had before.

"It's a three bedroom, two and half bath. Has a two car garage. It's near me and Haden. We have an opening here. The school is great. Please."

Damn she was very persuasive. I finally nodded.

"Good. We're going to be in each other's lives. We should be friendly. Especially for the kids' sake's. They have many brothers and sisters. Cousins. Aunts. Uncles. Grandparents."

"What are you saying?"

I looked at Addyson and hoped I'd looked as confused as I felt. "Did Haden tell you why I wasn't with him?"

"No."

"When I was sixteen years old, my boyfriend raped me. I got pregnant and was forced to give her up. It ate at me, but I was sixteen and didn't think I had a choice."

"Oh, my."

"I never told Haden. Not for a long time. About eight years ago he was shot and nearly died. I was told he had. He took the opportunity to find her and bring her home."

"Wow."

"I can't be mad that he slept with other women while he was traveling. I can't be mad he has other children besides ours. I have been with others and had children besides ours. I honestly don't know why this is bothering me so much."

"I wish I could understand."

"So do I." I looked at Addyson. "Let me gather a few things and you can follow me to the house."

"Sure."

I got up and left her office; taking a seat in the waiting room that was now empty as it was after hours.

I still had to call Teri and Hope. I'd do that later. That was going to be a very heavy conversation. Right now, this moment was important. Very important.

Chapter 12

I followed Addyson for about twenty minutes before finally pulling up to a beautiful 2 story, 2 car garage home. It was a deep blue with gray trim and a light gray door.

"Wow!" Alexa exclaimed. "I can't afford this."

"The rent is cheap," I replied. "Here."

Addyson held out a set of keys.

"What?"

"Finish out the school year here. Don't worry about rent. I'll pay you a good wage. The electric and other utilities are all you have to worry about."

"But..."

I don't deserve this. I need to tell her that I'm not staying.

I'm a drug addict.

I'm an alcoholic.

I don't deserve this. My kids do, but I don't. Not at all. I needed to tell her the truth.

"Look, it won't be easy. I have a lot to work through, but I don't want to lose Haden. I don't want Haden to lose Bayley and Roman. I don't want them to lose him. We can make this work."

"All right. Can the kids stay with you while I go get our things?"

"Of course."

"This is temporary."

"Got it."

"I'll bring the kids in a couple of days. I'll be as quick as possible."

"No rush. Be safe. Once you get settled you can start work."

I nodded and took the keys, "Won't the owner be mad?"

"Nope."

I looked at Addyson. "Are you sure?"

"Yep. Haden and I own it."

"Okay. Are there more?"

"Let's go inside. We can sit. It's fully furnished."

* * *

"So?" Addyson asked

"I think so," I replied. "No. I know so. He's too good looking and too good at it."

I smiled and caught myself.

Addyson smiled then. "It's okay. He is. There's no denying it."

"I'm sorry."

She shrugged. "I do want us to get along."

"I'd like that. I don't want any awkwardness. I should have done this years ago. I'm sorry."

"It's not you. It's me. I don't get why it hurts so much. Like I said we have an open marriage. We had an open relationship prior to being married."

"Is it guilt? Yours, because of your past?"

"Could be." I shrugged again. "I'll get over it."

"No matter how many?"

Addyson laughed. "Once we know each other better there's so much I can tell you."

I laughed this time and didn't hide it. She was really easy to get along with. Very kind. Nice. "Okay."

"We'd better get going. I have a case to get going."

"I need to get the kids."

We both got into our respective cars and drove in opposite directions. I knew my kids were at her house, but I wanted to get them dinner.

There was a bar nearby. I needed to stop and have a couple of beers. The bars I'd found here so far had been very generous with their pours.

I was going to try and stay away from the hard stuff today. I'd be by myself soon enough. I'd have enough time to indulge then.

Chapter 13

Two days later, I left. Bayley and Roman weren't happy, but they knew that they'd be safe and could get to know their dad. More of their family. I had been an only child and my parents had passed away long before the twins were born.

I couldn't face Teri and Hope today, so I stayed the same hotel in Delta Park that I'd stayed at with Roman and Bayley. I needed to give Teri and Hope a heads up. I needed a breather. This was also the first time, besides yesterday, that I've had to myself in eight years.

After I checked int, I went to the nearest liquor store and bought some Fireball and Pinnacle vodka. It was birthday cake flavored.

I had to be careful with my cocaine and heroin. I still had enough to hold me until I got home. I would have to find someone here to me, if I did come back. I knew I wasn't going to though. I don't know why I was thinking about.

I really needed to get back and talk to to Teri and Hope.

There was so much that I had to tell them. I hoped they'd listen.

* * *

"Hope? Teri?" I asked. I thought my phone had dropped the call. "Hello?"

"We're here," Hope said.

"You're leaving us?" Teri said, obviously pissed. "For strangers?"

"His wife begged me stay. To keep the kids close by. She's going to give me a house and a job. I don't think I'll take the job. Please, don't be mad. You two should come up, too. They asked for you to come."

"Where are you?"

"Right now, I'm in Portland, Oregon. I wanted a day alone. To prepare."

I had my shoes off and had a filled a syringe while I'd been talking to them. I bent over and injected the heroin between my toes. That felt so good.

"Prepare for what?"

"A six hour drive alone."

"To get the courage to tell us?"

I sighed. "Yes. I want you to come up with me. Like said, they want you up here, too. I'm sure they can help you find a house and jobs. There are tons of hotels and other businesses. Plus the kids will have a ton of family."

"Our families..."

"Hope, your family is in Oregon anyway, but we know that once you told them about being a single mother living with other single mothers they didn't want you around. I'm saying it to be mean, just truthful. Teri..."

"I know."

"I'll be home either late tonight or early tomorrow. Pleas, just think about it."

"Fine."

They hung up and I laid down.

* * *

I took a nap, but the sleep didn't last long enough. I needed to call Haden and check in. I, at least, had to pretend to care for a little longer.

I picked my phone up and called Haden.

"Hello?" he asked, answering.

"Good evening," I said. "May I speak with Bayley or Roman."

"Sure."

He called to the twins. I could hear them running towards the phone.

"Mommy!" Roman exclaimed.

"Hi, love," I said, tearing up. Was I making a mistake? "How are you?"

"Good. Been having fun. So many brothers and sisters!"

"You're listening?"

"Yes."

"Okay. Let me talk to your sister."

I heard them pass the phone. "Mommy!" she said. "Did you know that I have nieces and nephews?!"

"No, little miss, I didn't. That's so cool."

Chapter 14

February 6, 2019

Shasta Mountains, California

I walked into my childhood home and heard five sets of little feet running towards me. I braced myself.

"Auntie Alexa! Auntie Alexa!" Emilia Rose, Hope's oldest daughter, called.

"Where's Bayley?" Aurora asked.

"Where's Roman?" Donovan Haden asked.

"He's in Washington, they both are."

"Why?" Victoria asked.

"Yeah, why, Auntie Alexa?" Sadie Mallory asked. "With who?"

"Don't worry about it," Teri said, standing behind them in the hall.

"Okay, Mommy."

"Go play," Hope added.

They flew into the dining room where we had their playroom set up.

Hope turned her attention to me, arms crossed. "So?" she asked.

I wasn't feeling very well suddenly. My arms felt heavy. It felt like there was something sitting on my chest. I had the near uncontrollable urge to cough.

"So, what?" I replied, trying to fight the feeling.

"Are we going to talk about this?" Teri asked.

"You, neither of you, have to leave. Haden asked that you come so he could meet his kids. Our kids have been raised together, but they have other siblings."

"What do you mean? How does he know about us?"

"Haden and his wife have a bunch of kids. Some biological, some adopted. Some alive, some deceased. Tessa is the eldest and lives in California with her husband. Melody is the youngest. They have two grandchildren."

"So?"

"Why would we deny Haden a chance to see his children? At least, now that we know where he is."

"He…"

This pain in my chest was getting worse. I couldn't smell anything either. That was really bothering me. "Did nothing wrong. Neither did we. I told his wife that I'd be quick, but I'm not feeling well. I'm going to lay down. A lot has happened in a couple of days."

"Cold? Hey, are you okay?"

I shrugged. "It really hit me as I pulled in. Got worse while we were talking. Achy. A little hard to breath. It feels like there is an elephant sitting on my chest."

"Hope, can you watch the kids? I'm taking her to the hospital. With that new illness going around, best to not take any chances," Teri said.

"Of course."

"Please, Hope, really think about going. It will be good for them."

Hope nodded. "Okay."

"Please?"

"I promise."

"Thank you."

Maybe I should have been taking this COVID-19 thing seriously. It literally felt like something was sitting on my chest. Elephant? I don't know. I just didn't feel good and didn't like how I was feeling.

* * *

When Teri and I arrived at the hospital, it was very busy. We were asked to put face masks on. There were people that were coughing and moaning in the waiting room.

Teri helped me get checked in since I was having a difficult time catching my breath. I didn't need oxygen yet, but probably soon. I asked her if she wanted to leave.

"Of course not," she replied. "Do you really think that there will be room for us in Haden's life?"

"Yes," I replied. "I spoke with his wife, Addyson, for a couple of hours. She knew that he'd slept around. They have an open marriage. She's got kids with other men. Though, she's having a tough time with him having kids with someone else."

"Why?"

I shrugged and it hurt. Man this came out of nowhere. "She wasn't sure. Addyson is a strong woman."

"Why was he without her when he came through?"

"Ms. Down?" the nurse called.

"Can my friend come?" I asked, standing.

"For now."

Teri stood and we took a very long walk to get to a room.

Chapter 15

The nurse asked Teri to step outside briefly while she did an exam. I thought that was a little odd for a breathing problem, but what did I know?

As she checked me over, she asked, "How long have you been using drugs?"

"Years," I said. "I've forgotten how many."

"I had a feeling and that's why I asked your friend to stand in the hallway. I didn't want to embarrass you. She can come in now. I'll let her know when I go."

"Thank you."

The nurse nodded and finished taking my vitals, before leaving and sending Teri back in.

"So?" Teri asked. "Why?"

"He was shot, like his school had said," I replied. I wasn't breathing much better, so the nurse put me on oxygen. I had a bad feeling that I would be put on an IV next. "He took the time to find her daughter."

"Why was she missing? Why didn't this Addyson look, too?"

"He wanted to surprise her. I guess he didn't want to get her hopes up in case things didn't work out. Like he couldn't find her or she didn't want to go back with him. Addyson had been raped when she was sixteen years old by her boyfriend. She got pregnant. Her parents forced her to give the baby up. She always regretted it."

"Wow. She sounds amazing."

"Seems to be."

Teri looked at me suddenly. "Are you okay?"

I shook my head. "No."

She rushed to the bed and hit the button to call for the nurse.

The doctor and nurse came in to shove a large cotton swab up my nose. They went really far up with that thing. I think I felt it in my brain! The swab was sent off and I was getting really warm. I felt like I had a high fever. It seemed like it took forever for them to get the results back.

"Miss?" the nurse said, looking at Teri. "You need to leave."

"Why?" I asked, scared.

"You have COVID-19. It is highly contagious. You need to go get tested and have your family tested if she's been around them recently. You can call her on the phone or come visit when she's in isolation."

Teri nodded and I think she actually looked relieved. Did she know about my drug use? My alcohol use?

Chapter 16

February 8, 2019

I had been calling Haden or Addyson everyday to speak with the twins. I'd lost track of how long I'd been in here. I finally decided that it was about time to get my phone disconnected, but first I had a request of Teri and hope.

"You're not dead!" Teri protested. She was on the phone. I wasn't allowed visitors, because of how contagious this was. "You're abandoning your children with strangers!"

"I know," I said, starting to cry. "Just tell him that my family doesn't want the twins. Go to him. To them. Promise me."

"Fine. Fine. We'll go, but *when* you get better you have to explain why you lied."

"Of course."

"Why *are* you lying, anyway?"

I sighed and coughed. "If I do, heaven forbid, die; I don't want my kids to watch that happen."

"I see."

"You've been a great friend and a great mother. Hope, too."

I was saying goodbye. Teri had other plans.

"Stop, Alexa. We knew. We've always known."

"About what?" I said, looking at my phone.

"About the drugs and alcohol. You were good at hiding it, but we made sure the kids ate. Had new clothes."

"Teri..."

"I knew when you'd drink at work. No one else did. You were a great boss, like I said, when you weren't drinking. You're a great mother, too. We won't take the kids in. We love them like their our own, but we *do* have our own kids to think about."

"Teri..."

"Don't worry, we'll tell Haden and Addyson that you died. We'll lie for you. One last time. I do want to say, that you're being a coward."

Teri hung up and I called Hope.

Chapter 17

February 10, 2019

"Bayley!" I exclaimed. "How's my big girl doing? Keeping an eye on your brother?"

"Yes, Mommy," she said. "Hanging out with Daddy has been fun."

"You're behaving for your Daddy and Addyson."

"Yes. She's really nice. We have cousins!"

"That's great." I coughed. "Let me talk to your brother. I love you."

"I love you, too. Roman! Roman!"

"Mommy?" he asked.

"Hi, baby," I replied, tearing up. Soon I'd disconnect my phone. I was being a chicken again. I know that it needed to be done. I just needed a couple of more phone calls. This was going to be one of the last phone calls I made to him. "How are you?"

"Good. We have a new sister! She's mine and Bayley's age, too. She looks like Aurora and Victoria!"

"How?"

"I don't know. Addyson can tell you. Did Bayley tell you that she's fun?"

"Yes." I felt a stab of jealousy. They were mine not hers! They weren't even going to miss me! "You're listening to Daddy and Addyson?"

"Of course. I'm a good boy." I laughed. He sounded so offended that I'd actually believe otherwise. "We have another brother, too. He's our age. He gets scared sometimes, but I love him a lot."

"Why does he get scared?"

"I don't know. Want to talk to him?"

"No..."

"Ben! My mommy wants to talk you." I heard some mumbles. "She wants to know why you get scared. Well, I can't tell her. I don't know why."

"Roman..."

"Hello?" a small unfamiliar voice said.

"Hi," I replied. "Are you Ben?"

"Yeah."

"I'm Alexa. Roman and Bayley's mom."

"Hi."

"Why are you scared?"

"When I was three years old I was in a fire. No burns. I was protected. My older brothers, Milo and Elliott. Didn't make it. Neither did my older sisters, Willow and Amethyst. Then a firefighter took me away. I still have nightmares. I scare the other kids. I wake up screaming sometimes."

"That's horrible."

"Here's Roman."

"Bye, Mommy! Here's Bayley." I heard the phone change hands, running feet. "Ben!"

"Addyson wants to talk to you."

"Sure."

"Addyson! Mommy is ready to talk to you!"

The phone changed hands again and I braced myself.

Chapter 18

"How are you feeling, Alexa?" Addyson asked. "The twins miss you."

"I'm okay," I replied. Actually, I was getting worse. I thought it would pass, but it wasn't. I don't think that I'll be around much longer. "Getting worse. The oxygen helps a little."

"What does the doctor say?"

"Not much. I mainly see the nurses. I've lost weight. It's so difficult to eat, because of the coughing. Sometimes, I vomit. I don't think they're very optimistic."

"What hospital?"

I started coughing and had to hang up. I didn't want them to know where I was.

* * *

After I stopped coughing, I called my phone company.

"Thank you for calling Verizon," the voice said. "This is Bob. How may I help you?"

"I'd like to disconnect my service please," I said.

"I'm sorry to hear that. What's the phone number and name on the account?"

"Alexa Downs." I gave him my phone number. "I can be sent the final bill. I just need to cancel."

"Of course, ma'am. I need you social security number and an email address to send you the cancellation information."

I gave him both.

"Thank you. Please bear with me."

I heard the keys of his keyboard.

"Ms. Downs, you are asking Verizon Wireless to cancel your service today. Your final bill with the early cancellation fee is going to be $500.20. Do you wish to proceed?"

"Yes."

"Would you like the bill emailed to you or a paper bill?"

"It doesn't matter."

"You need to pick one."

I started coughing. I don't know why it mattered. "Email."

"Are you okay, ma'am?"

"No. I have COVID."

"I'm sorry."

"Thank you." I hung up and called for the nurse.

Chapter 19

The next day, I used the hospital phone to call a lawyer and then my maternal grandparents.

"What do you want, Alexa?" my grandfather, Steven, asked.

"Where are you?" my grandmother, Mindy, asked. "What number is this? It isn't your cell or the house number."

"I'm in the hospital," I replied.

My Grandfather sighed. "Did you OD?"

"No."

"What's going on?"

"I have COVID. It's bad, Grandma."

"How bad?"

"Bad." As if I needed to demonstrate, I had a bad coughing fit that lasted a few minutes.

"Oh. No. What about the kids?"

Here's the thing. When they'd found out that I was pregnant and that I was going to be a single mother; they weren't happy. They said that my parents would be disappointed in me. Once they held Bayley and Roman for the first time, their only great-grandchildren, they fell in love.

I still needed to all my paternal grandparents about me being in the hospital.

"I found their father. They're with him and his wife. I need a favor. Two, maybe."

"His wife?"

"Grandpa, please?"

"Sorry. Go ahead."

"I know that the trust only takes care of the house while I'm living it, but I know you could talk to the lawyer and change that, right?"

"Yes."

"If I die…"

"Don't say that." My maternal grandparents are tough people. They've lived a rough life and fought to get what our family has, but they did love me. Faults and all. I didn't know why. "Don't say that."

"If I die, please keep the house going. Don't let the lawyer sell it."

"Why?"

"I have two friends that were in the same situation as me. Not the drugs and alcohol, but the single mother thing. We all moved in together before the kids were born. We've been raising the kids together. I took Bayley and Roman to their father. If they do the same, please, then sell the house. Or whatever you need to do. I don't want Hope and Teri to leave their home. Teri has twins like me, and Hope has triplets."

"We won't."

"I'll give you their numbers so that you can keep in touch. Thank you. One more thing?"

"What?"

"Please don't look for the twins. Leave them be."

"Depends."

"On what?"

"Are they safe? Tell us about their father and his wife."

"Their father is a good man. He loves his children and wife."

"He loves her? He cheated on her!"

I smiled and started coughing again. "Sorry. They have an open marriage."

"Oh. Why was he here? Why wasn't she with him?"

I knew that was coming. "He had gotten shot; I don't know the details. Long story short, he faked his death so that he could find her daughter."

"Why?"

"He didn't want her to be disappointed if the girl didn't want to come with him or if he didn't find her."

"Why wasn't she with her mother?"

"She was the product of a rape. His wife had wanted to keep her, but she was forced to give her up. She was only sixteen years old and regretted that she didn't just runaway when she found out."

"Wow."

"He was a teacher and principal. Then he owned a bar. She was a police officer and now runs a private detective agency."

"The kids are safe?"

"Yes. Lots of family around."

"We won't look for them. For now. We promise that we won't try to take them away."

"Thank you. I need to rest before I call Daddy's parents."

"Do you…"

"No. I need to do it. I have a lawyer coming by to do a will. I don't have much, but I want to leave Hope and Teri what I do have. I'm going to put in the will that they don't have to leave unless they want to."

"Okay. Have your lawyer send us whatever we need to sign. We'll sign it."

"Thank you. I love you. Goodbye."

"Bye."

I replaced the receiver and instantly fell asleep.

Chapter 20

February 12, 2019

I had slept the rest of the eleventh away and woke up too early to call my other grandparents or check in with the lawyer to find out what time he was coming in.

I called for the nurse. I hadn't eaten all day yesterday and was a little hungry.

"Yes?" she asked, entering the room with a hazmat looking suit. "Are you okay?"

"Could I get some pudding or Jello?" I asked. "Some water?"

"Of course. Breakfast will be up in a couple of hours."

"Thank you."

* * *

The lawyer wasn't able to show up in person. So, the hospital brought me in a laptop, so that I culd speak with the lawyer via video chat.

"I don't have a lot, but what I have I want to go to my roommates," I said, breathing heavily.

"Fine," he said. "Kids?"

"Twins. Roman and Bayley. I'm not leaving them anything. They are with their father and will want for nothing I don't want my friends to leave the house. It's taken care of my a trust that is overseen by my maternal grandparents and a lawyer. When my parents died they wanted to make sure that I always had a place to live. I was into drugs and alcohol. Whatever you need for my grandparents to sign they will."

I gave him their address and phone number.

"Fine."

"How long will this take to complete?"

"It's fairly simple. I'll draft it up and send the papers to your grandparents, but it depends on how long it takes them to sign it after their lawyer takes a look.”

“Okay. I need it done quickly.”

“Will there be a DNR?”

“Yes.”

“Fine. The hospital can take care of that.”

“Fine.” Dick. “Just have it sent to me here at the hospital when it’s ready for me to sign.”

“Fine.”

I closed the laptop and called for a nurse to take it.

While I waited, I called my paternal grandparents.

Chapter 21

"Who is this?" my grandmother, Lauren, asked.

"Alexa," I replied, trying not to cough.

"Oh. Where are you? This isn't the house number is it? Or you cell phone?"

"Where's Grandpa?"

"Getting ready for work. Where are you?"

"The hospital."

"Did you overdose again?"

"No, ma'am. I have COVID. It's bad. I just spoke with a lawyer."

"No!"

I heard something fall and then running and yelling.

"Who the hell is this? What did you tell my wife?" my grandfather, Sonny, demanded. "She fainted!"

"Is she okay?"

"Yes. Who is this?"

"It's Alexa. I told her that I'm in the hospital with COVID. I met with a lawyer."

"Oh, God. Where are the kids? Did *those* people take them?"

"No, sir. Before I got sick, I took them to their father. I found him. He and his wife took them in. Is Grandma okay?"

"Yes. Yes. She's coming around. His wife?"

"Yes."

I told him everything that I'd told my other grandparents. "I have a favor to ask."

"What's that?"

"Please, don't look for the kids. They are safe and loved. This is the best thing for them. Don't try to get custody."

"They're our great-grandchildren! We..."

"Told me, just like Mom's parents, that I should get rid of them. That Mom and Dad would have been disappointed in me."

"You got knocked up and weren't married! You didn't know anything about the father!"

I started coughing. "Please. Promise me!"

"Okay. The house..."

"Will be kept up by the trust. My friends and their kids are living there. Mom's parents agreed."

"Fine. Fine."

"I love you. I'm sorry that I was a disappointment. That I caused so much trouble."

"It was no trouble. We love you, too."

"I have to go."

"Your Grandmother wants to say something."

"Okay." I heard them as they passed the phone. "Hi, Grandma?"

"I love you, Alexa. You were a wonderful granddaughter. A wonderful daughter. A wonderful mother. Your parents loved you. I know you had your faults, but we all do. I feel very privileged to have been your grandmother."

I started to cry. "Goodbye."

Epilogue

"I, Alexa Downs, being of sound mind and body leave the following:

"To my friend, Hope, I leave the house. The trust will stay open to keep with the upkeep as it always has. You will be able to stay there as long as you need.

"To my friend, Teri, I leave the house. The trust will stay open to keep with the upkeep as it always has. You will be able to stay there as long as you need.

"To their children: Victoria, Aurora, Sadie Mallory, Donovan Haden, and Emilia Rose; I leave the house. The trust will stay open to keep with the upkeep as it always has. You will be able to stay there as long as you need.

"To my children, Bayley and Roman; I leave you nothing. You are better off without me. Please know

that I did love you. That's why I went to find your father after so long. I should have done it sooner.

"Hope, Teri; please don't keep the kids away from their father. You know where he is. I left his information. If you decide to move and live where he does, the house will then be sold. Tell my grandparents after you've gotten everything out of the house.

"To all of my grandparents; I'm sorry for all the trouble I caused to you and my parents. I loved you all.

"Peace. Love. Hope. Respect. Mercy.

"Here I come, Mommy and Daddy."

Signed,

Alexa Downs

81

Acknowledgments

I just want to thank those of you who helped me go over this piece with a fine-tooth comb. I also want to thank my co-workers for putting up with how often I said aloud how many words I had written and how many I had left to go. Thank you for encouraging me while I wrote this!

Also enjoy these other novels from Marie Garcia

Delta Files

The Hotel Slayings

The Masked Killer

Ballerina

Recreational Murder

Fake

Trea-Bella Donna

Vacay

Trea-Bella Donna: Prison Queen

Suicide Killer

State Route

Coroner

Addyson

Broken

Redemption

Untold Stories

Haden Delta, Volume 1

Tessa Kellogg

Tessa Kellogg-Easter, Volume 2

Addyson's Memories

Conception

A Chance Meeting

Poetry Collections

Bored and Bleeding

Egotistical Mama

Powerful Desire

From Me to You

Blood Speaks

Remembrance

Sinking Freely

Weeping Summer

Coast to Coast

Random Designs

Short Story Collections

The Scorned American

A Perfectly Secret Affair

The Haunted Third Shift

Lonely Nights and Crimson Lips

Worlds Apart and Then Some

Second Sapphire

Deadly

Key Moments

Stranded Feelings

2 in 1 Novels

Espionage Garden

Hotels Unmasked

Recreational Ballet

A Marvelous Black Death

Vacant Queen

Killer State

The Duo

The Ending

For Better or Worse

Specialty Novels

2030

Writing Death

Black Widow

Marvelous

Sai

Gypsy Rose

Other Novels

Dew

Weird

Twelve Months

Better Days

Espionage: An American Tale

The Garden

Dreamland Theater

Almost Amish

Come Travel with Me

Black Widow

A Far Worse Place (Vol. 1)

Wastelands

A Better Worse Place (Vol. 2)

The Expectant Mother

The Photography Sessions

The Evil Ones

About the Author

Marie was born in Modesto, California in September of 1981 and raised in Vancouver, Washington. She graduated high school from Prairie High School in Brush Prairie, Washington in June of 2000. In January of 2006 she graduated college from Everest College (formerly Western Business College) in Vancouver, Washington.

She was raised by her maternal grandparents and has five half sisters and two half brothers.

Marie married in the fall of 2010 and they reside in Pennsylvania.